for abigail - dm
for mom, dad and ali- nw

Text copyright 2005 © Dan Manalang
Illustrations copyright 2005 © Nichole Wong

Book designed by Nichole Wong
Text in this book is set in URWAntiquaTOT
The illustrations for this book are rendered digitally

First Edition
2 4 6 8 10 9 7 5 3 1

Library of Congress
Cataloging-in-Publication data available

ISBN 0 9769342 0 5
Published by Flip Publishing
P.O. Box 1072
Hawthorne, CA 90251

Printed in China
Distributed by flip Publishing

Ambrosia

Words by **Dan Manalang**
Illustrations by **Nichole Wong**

Publishing

A funny thing happened

at the market today.

It happened in the fruit section where the fruits were at play.

There were cherries cheering, watermelons warbling,

raspberries rappin', and lemons laughing.

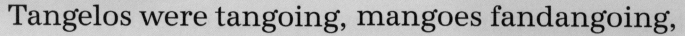

Tangelos were tangoing, mangoes fandangoing,

figs jigging, and guavas tinikling.

* Tinikling - the national dance of the Philippines that involves graceful dance movements in between bamboo sticks.

Purple plums were plummeting,

tangerines tumbling,

bananas bashing,

and papayas dashing.

There were berries flipping through the air,

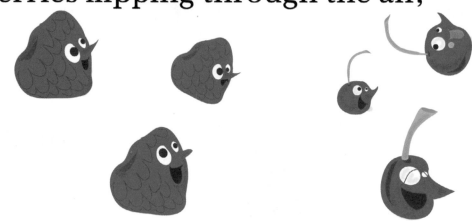

and pears leaping without fear.

When suddenly something fell from the sky.

It was round, brown, and
had dark eyes.

What could it be?

Where did it come from? Nobody knew.

"It's certainly not one of us,"
the pineapple pompously accused.

The curious banana asked,
"What might you be?"

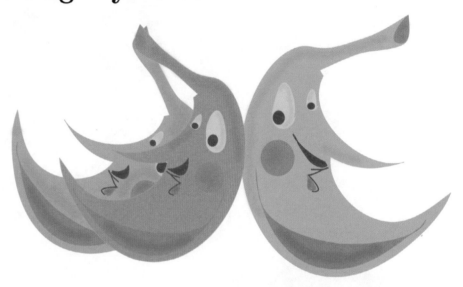

He declared, "I am a coconut,
I am what you see."

"You're round, brown and hairy," said the strawberry.

" You're round, brown and scary," whimpered the quivering cherry.

"On the contrary, I'm just like you, a fruit," confessed the coconut.

"Fruit or no fruit, I think you're rather cute," proclaimed the peach.

The coconut construed, "I grew up on a warm sandy beach

in a tall skinny tree, on a tropical island
of the Philippines, and proud to be."

The grumpy grape uttered, with little regard,
"You can't be a fruit, your shell is too hard."

The coconut silently smiled removing his shell to discard.

He revealed he was smooth as an apple, crisp and clean,

he was as juicy as an orange, but his juice was sweet milky cream.

The blueberry took one taste then blushed with blue,

she smirked at the grumpy grape and declared, "He's sweeter than you."

They took turns partaking of the coconut and were very well pleased.

Convinced he was a fruit, they all happily agreed.

A valuable lesson was revealed
to all that day,

They truly believed what
the coconut had to say.

"You must never judge a fruit by the color
of its skin," he humbly said,

"or where it came from or where it has been."

"What truly matters always comes from within."